Parents and Caregivers,

Stone Arch Readers are designed to provide enjoyable reading experiences, as well as opportunities to develop vocabulary, literacy skills, and comprehension. Here are a few ways to support your beginning reader:

- Talk with your child about the ideas addressed in the story.

- Discuss each illustration, mentioning the characters, where they are, and what they are doing.

- Read with expression, pointing to each word. You may want to read the whole story through and then revisit parts of the story to ensure that the meanings of words or phrases are understood.

- Talk about why the character did what he or she did and what your child would do in that situation.

- Help your child connect with characters and events in the story.

Remember, reading with your child should be fun, not forced. Each moment spent reading with your child is a priceless investment in his or her literacy life.

Gail Saunders-Smith, Ph.D.

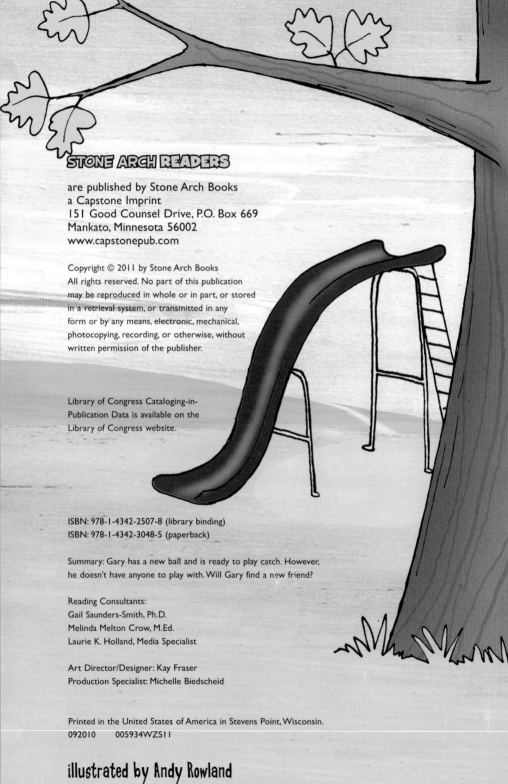

STONE ARCH READERS

are published by Stone Arch Books
a Capstone Imprint
151 Good Counsel Drive, P.O. Box 669
Mankato, Minnesota 56002
www.capstonepub.com

Library of Congress Cataloging-in-
Publication Data is available on the
Library of Congress website.

ISBN: 978-1-4342-2507-8 (library binding)
ISBN: 978-1-4342-3048-5 (paperback)

Summary: Gary has a new ball and is ready to play catch. However,
he doesn't have anyone to play with. Will Gary find a new friend?

Reading Consultants:
Gail Saunders-Smith, Ph.D.
Melinda Melton Crow, M.Ed.
Laurie K. Holland, Media Specialist

Art Director/Designer: Kay Fraser
Production Specialist: Michelle Biedscheid

Printed in the United States of America in Stevens Point, Wisconsin.
092010   005934WZS11

illustrated by Andy Rowland

Little Lizard's
NEW FRIEND

by Melinda Melton Crow

STONE ARCH BOOKS
a capstone imprint

This is Dad Lizard.
This is Mom Lizard.
This is Gary Lizard.

It was a nice day.

Gary had a new ball.

"Will you play ball with me?"
said Gary.

"I'm busy," said Dad.

13

"Will you play ball with me?"
said Gary.

"I'm busy,"
said Mom.

"Who will play ball with me?" said Gary.

"I will," said Frog.

"You will?" said Gary.

"Yes. I like to play ball," said Frog.

"Oh boy!" said Gary.
"I have a new friend."

27

"So do I," said Frog.

Gary and his new friend
played ball all day.

STORY WORDS

nice	ball	frog
day	busy	friend

Total Word Count: 93